When I Return To You, I Will Be Unfed is a poignant, gritty exploration of mental illness and one man's search for safe haven. Bowen's unflinching prose grips the reader and doesn't let go until the final, perfect beat of narrative. This book may be short in length, but it will remain with the reader long after it ends.

—James Claffey, author of *Blood a Cold Blue*

This is a quiet though powerful tale of the vagaries of the human spirit in the face of physical, emotional and spiritual opposition. The juxtaposition of nature and medicine as the subtext of healing our lives is handled with sensitive finesse. The power of a great story without gimmick or emotional manipulation is both a rare and beautiful thing to experience.

—Michelle Reale, author and
Associate Professor at Arcadia University

Christopher Bowen wrings more meaning from a sentence than most writers do from whole stories. This richly complex story brings Bowen's linguistic skills to bear on psychology and personal trauma, crafting a narrative both deeply emotional and intellectual. Every line bears layered meaning, playing on the narrator's complicated view of himself and his world. In this way, Bowen has managed to write a story that feels like a novel.

—Sam Snoek-Brown, author of *Box Cutters*
and the forthcoming *Where There Is Ruin*

When I Return To You, I Will Be Unfed

CHRISTOPHER BOWEN

Acknowledgments

Portions of information used in this text, specifically those pertaining to the clinical delineation of depression and psychiatry, have been provided courtesy of the American Psychiatric Association and their website.

Special thanks to Nancy Stohlman for her copy editing and general manuscript commentary.

Book Design by David McNamara.

"There came a time when the risk
to remain tight in the bud was more painful
than the risk it took to blossom."

—*Anaïs Nin*

Jim was taken and not the way anyone saw coming. I think of the white clouds and breath and the white van parked outside, the kind of cargo van repairmen drive only no ladders on it. Then I think how he was taken higher than the honey bees, past cell phone towers, past rolling Ohio farmland into a custody, an expansive mind meant to be free, but committed to me as a friend.

"Tell me your name and we'll go from there."

"My name is James, James Nichols."

"Do you know why you're here?"

"No, I don't."

"It's because you've been too strong for too long, Jim. Have you heard of a poem called *Footprints*?"

"No."

"It goes to say that looking back over that sandy beach where once there were two sets of footprints then there were only one. The author asks, 'Dear Lord, why was there only one set at times? I thought you were walking beside me always.' And the Lord replies, 'Because it was then that I carried you.' It's time to let someone carry you, Jim."

I follow the light breath in the folding dusk, dark footprints crackling into colored, fall leaves from last year. Jim is gone. All the honey bees, they are gone.

Bipolar disorder is defined by three categories: bipolar I, bipolar II and cyclothymic disorder. Bipolar I disorder can cause dramatic mood swings. Bipolar I disorder is diagnosed when a person has a manic episode.

During a manic episode, people with bipolar disorder may feel on top of the world or uncomfortably irritable. During a depressive episode they may feel sad and hopeless.

I stretch the night away from me like a blanket and stretch that blanket. The flimsy, photocopied paper, the doctor said it would help me understand this. I think there's a ghost in the room, an invisible person, so I check under the bed coming up with my hands clasped praying and holding poetry, the expansion of south Cleveland outside my ninth story window. It's dark with streetlights like fireflies. The steam rises from sewer covers away and down from my room and I think I am rising. They shave me. I rise. It's morning. I rise. I don't know why they do. I don't know why I do. I didn't think I had razors and if I did if I was trying to grow out the faint upper lip. Somehow they come into my room and shave me and the doctor visits.

"One more day, just give it one more day."

I ask if I'm on vacation from school. He says, yes. A man comes in and gives me a handful of pills. Blue and green. Like an ocean. I swallow them with water. He says good, they are good, I should rest because supper will be here soon. Drool stretches from my chin late that afternoon. There's no television and I'm told if I want to watch I have to go to the community room.

"Am I allowed to leave?"

It's my second or third day, maybe my birthday. The drool dries. The doctor says yes, says he has a meeting, has to go himself. I yearn to follow him with an invisible briefcase looking the way his does, dark brown with soft leather.

"I have a meeting," I tell the nurse.

He gives me my medication. I ask him if he knows where or who it's with. He shakes his head. It's morning again.

"I don't either," I say.

I have a friend and there's a man somewhere leaving footprints.

Mood stabilizers are the most commonly prescribed type of medication for bipolar disorder. Anticonvulsant medications are also sometimes used. In psychotherapy, the individual can work with a psychiatrist or other mental health professional to work out problems, better understand the illness and rebuild relationships. A psychiatrist is also able to prescribe medications as part of a treatment plan.

"I can't believe I'm actually defending the E.M.T. on this."

"But Rob, Jim was fine. He'd been acting nutty, but that's Jim."

"He wasn't fine. Everyone in his dorm said they hadn't seen him for weeks, that he stayed up throughout the night, and that there were myth he never left."

"Well, I pray you're right."

At parties, if and when Jim came to them, he would run around as if drunk before anyone had even gotten there. Later in the night, he would talk slurred gibberish—something about stars on his dorm walls at night, a moon, a map. He drew there. I thought he was doing drugs. Something had changed inside him. The white van, the hospital, I wished for Jim with me on that walk from the dorm when they'd finally come—the white, white breath.

Honey bees are one of the only insects that once they've stung, die off. When I was a child, Jim's father showed me this, not by being masculine about it and stinging himself, but when I walked across Jim's lawn covered in clover, I'd gotten stung. Bee stings also cause high levels of antibodies. Enough of it over the course of time and you can become immune. After the shock of the sting, hobbling into the front door crying, he took my foot showing me the stinger. There was a sac attached to the end of it.

"That's where the bee keeps his 'poison,'" he said.

"Does that mean I'm going to die?"

"No, their poison is just a way to hurt or warn you. It's only useful on other bugs," he laughed.

"What's poison?"

When I met his grandma—a tree that had seen centuries pass around it, circles of lifelines of a cut oak or cedar—she would sit in her chair all day in the living room drinking tea or juice reading and watching those years and people pass growing those circles. What did she see between the lines there?

I remember Jim telling me about sleeping on the couch across from her when he was home from college and waking up in the morning to her glasses peering over the brim of a newspaper at him.

The doctor says visiting isn't an option until a week or two has passed, his family at least have some time to soak this in themselves. He said to wait until Jim called.

I knew Jim was sad. How deep the river ran, I don't know. They say you only see ripples of rocks from rivers running deep enough. Sometimes, you see rapids.

Bipolar disorder can run in families. In fact, eighty to ninety percent of individuals with bipolar disorder have a relative with depression or bipolar disorder. Though environmental factors can also contribute to bipolar disorder, extreme stress, sleep disruption, and drugs or alcohol may trigger episodes in vulnerable patients.

A manic episode is a period of at least one week when a person is high spirited or irritable in an extreme way most of the day and for most days, has more energy than usual and experiences at least three of the following list:

- *Exaggerated self-esteem*
- *Less need for sleep*
- *Talking more than usual, loudly and quickly*
- *Easily distracted*
- *Doing many activities at once or scheduling*

more events in a day than can be accomplished

🐜 *Increased reckless behavior (e.g., careless driving, spending sprees)*

🐜 *Uncontrollable racing thoughts or quickly changing ideas or topics*

Changes are significant and clear to friends and family. Symptoms are severe enough to cause problems with work, family and social activities and responsibilities.

A manic episode may require a person to get hospital care.

I walk to the community room looking from the corner of my door both ways like the way my parents taught me to cross the street. There are people shuffling at a desk mid-hall, some dressed in uniforms, others in pajamas. I look both ways and walk towards the desk thinking no one will notice me. I thought I'd be able to walk the hallway on out to the far window up into the sky, but the nurse comes up to me quickly with a greeting. In confusion, I think he wants me back in the room. I look from him to the window and back, scared and upset, as he guides me to the desk.

"So, let's see what's going on here."

"Okay," I say.

I see what's real. They are holding me. The mind forms words I can't mouth, filtering them like oil on a car or water in a fish tank. It hasn't happened in a long time that I speak my mind.

"I'm going back to my room now to watch some TV. Is that okay?"

But speaking my mind is something to be proud of.

"Sure, sure Jim. Hope you are feeling better now. I'll be back in your room at lunch and maybe we can talk about your day then."

I return to my room where there is no television. It's still in the community room where I'd been told it was two days ago. I look through the open door of the room for people, but there are none. There is eternity, I have an opinion about it, and there is me.

Months walking this campus with Jim and still I never found the cemetery until now without him. I pass the library and park thinking of Civil

War soldiers—black and white photos, bayonettes, cannons, war. There are no squirrels here for some reason.

In another day or two he will call, I know it. From what his parents say he may be starting to understand he has an illness. I can't imagine Jim living that way, like someone schizophrenic or bi-polar, seeing and hearing things that aren't real, second guessing and racing thoughts—a war, a real, never-ending war. I wonder what people down the line will think, what people we knew from high school will think once they've met him after this. Who will he become?

It isn't completely dark and I would hate to be caught here alone. There are things caged and uncaged. There are criminals and there are patients. There are ones I see and there are ones that are waiting. I see the light, but what we wanted was the grave.

Jim took the trip to New Orleans to bring back voodoo dolls, blues records, and grave rubbings from the above-ground gravesites—the end result of a city below sea level. He had the charcoal and paper plastered all over his dorm room like a real artist, never giving them to me, and knowing it made me jealous. Something about stars and a map they say. Most went so far back you couldn't tell dates from names. They say there are three deaths in a person's life: the day they actually die, the day everyone that knew them has died, and the day the last person on earth speaks their name for the last time.

I met a woman, her hair straight and tied back, who looked a few years older than me. She woke me up from a dream in my hospital room sitting at the side of my bed in a plastic chair and lab coat in the morning with a notepad and pen the way Grandma used to read the paper. There were notes inside me.

"How are you feeling today?"

"Fine. May I ask who you are?" I rub my eyes.

"My name is Dr. Deitrich. I'm a resident under Dr. Newman. Do you like Dr. Newman?"

"Well, he's the only one who visits me here. So why are *you* here?"

"Just wanted to take some notes on what you think about this place and how you are feeling."

"Well, I don't like the food. The portions are too small."

I want to tell her I'm willing to hunger strike at the drop of a dime, that there are footprints just outside my bedroom window here, past the morning sun up farther. I'm a honey bee you know.

"Excuse me?"

I'm dying because I used to fly, but can't now. I feel sad some of the time. The sadness grows, covers my wings, my stinger, my honey. Maybe it is honey. I feel it and not in a good way. Am I trapped in this sweetness and is it compassion? Can you help me?

"Can you help me?" I ask.

"I don't understand. Help you with what?"

"Help me get out of here. The longer I stay here the sadder I get inside."

I think she will get me out but starts writing notes instead, her hands, slender fingers, moving with mechanical grace and fervor. She has a ring. She jotts the eternity onto the paper, the truth into words.

"I used to think sadness was bad. I'm starting to understand that sometimes it's good, that it's a part of me like this place somehow. Do you see this? It's so sad."

I reach into the drawer next to my bed, pulling out my paper copy of *Footprints*.

"I read this from time to time and it's so sad."

"What is it?"

"A poem."

I hand it to her, grateful that someone has asked about my situation, the sadness, my poem. There are watermarks on the gray copy paper where drops of tears have dried from random nights before, nights I stayed up with Cleveland.

"Oh, wow, this is interesting. Can I read it?"

"Yes, please."

"Who gave you this?"

"The doctor. Sometimes I really don't think he knows what's going on here with the people and stuff. There are crazy people here."

She chuckles to herself.

"Well, I think that's one of the reasons the doctor has brought you here: to figure out all these people and maybe your own sadness."

I like her and want her to visit again.

"Will you visit me every morning?"

She slides the paper across my bed, towards me and into my hand. I grip the blanket with the other pulling it tight, tighter than stretching the night, tighter than anything I've ever held onto in my life. I clench my teeth.

"I will try. I promise. I have to go now. Your breakfast will be here soon."

"You came to visit just me, didn't you? You came here just for me?"

"Yes, yes I did, Jim. And I promise I will be back."

When I return to you, I will be unfed.

A major depressive episode is a period of two weeks in which a person has at least five of the following symptoms, including one of the first two:

- *Intense sadness or despair; feeling helpless, hopeless or worthless*
- *Loss of interest in activities once enjoyed*
- *Feeling worthless or guilty*
- *Sleep problems—sleeping too little or too much*
- *Feeling restless or agitated (e.g., pacing or*

hand-wringing) or slowed speech or movements

🐜 Changes in appetite (increase or decrease)

🐜 Loss of energy, fatigue

🐜 Difficulty concentrating, remembering, making decisions

🐜 Frequent thoughts of death or suicide

Gary jumps up and down as we cross paths the first time down the hall clasping his hands together in exasperation and reaching his right one out to shake mine. I reach out and he vigorously shakes it. He is excited to meet me. I say hello and give him my name. He smiles, nodding his thin head, occasionally looking out of the corner of his eye as if something were there, but there isn't.

There are other people here in the halls, too. There's a woman who reminds me of Patti Smith with dark scraggly hair and a man a few years older than me who works construction. Another ethnic woman with a family of five or six who cries a lot, but we all wear pajamas.

I call Rob on the phone outside my room. They don't trust us with phones in our rooms, don't trust us with razors. They trust us with *Footprints*.

Trying to get through there's a girl my age breaking down on the other one down the same side of hall. She's slumped against the wall, her back to it, on the floor crying into the receiver. Her hands to her face, I ask Rob if he is still there. He says, yes. I say, I will be okay. He says, yes. I ask him to look after Christa. He says, yes.

I never see the girl from the phone down the hall again. Patti Smith and I play pool with a young Jewish kid who does yoga stretches in the hall and I'm reminded of my blanket.

"Why are you here?" she asks.

"I think it's because I'm kinda sad or, at least, staying here makes me feel like that."

"You must be really sad to be here then," she replies. "What have you been diagnosed with?"

I hesitate.

"I'm not diagnosed with anything, just trying to get outta here like the rest of us. I don't have an illness. Just trying to leave, you know?"

She laughs at this and we finish the pool game. She says they will keep me here as long as the man thinks they should and it makes her mad as hell.

It's the first thing I ask the doctor when he visits that afternoon, if he's the man.

"Not quite getting it, but sure. Actually, I'm starting to think that you're the man, Jim. We're going to start some new activities for you this week, group occupational activities and meeting with the team."

Okay, I say. It's best not to ask questions from the man.

I go to group. Gary is there. Dan the construction worker is there, even Patti Smith. We bake cookies and play board games. We joke about how Dan can't cook as he burns his cookie tray and Gary nods again smiling, though Dan takes the insult too seriously and can't laugh it off.

Gary continues to nod for the next five minutes before pointing to the empty seat next to him. I look into his eyes.

The occupational therapy lady that walks in every morning really gets me going, almost like an army drill sergeant. I think of the Jewish kid who does yoga and wonder how he feels about it, how he reacts to this woman coming into his room every morning because I think he is so much like me, and I remind myself to ask him.

"This is *my* room and I need to sleep," I yell to the doorway, dismissively.

I pull the blankets over my head trying to hide it. She is my mother waking me up for school. She says she will be back in fifteen minutes and that I better be ready for group. I slide the curtain that divides my half of it from my roommate. When I'm sure she's gone, I get dressed.

The strangest thing occurs to me when I walk down it. I have the feeling I am led by something inside as if I have the ambition today. Today I will bake cookies and they will be chocolate, my favorite, like every birthday cake I've ever had. I will share them, but where is my dorm room?

The morning sun hits my backside from the window at the end of the hall where the clouds were but they aren't now, the place I thought I could fly. They have started letting me wear normal clothes and the heat of the sun soaks through a favorite yellow t-shirt with a number seven on it I used to wear before going to bed and brushing my teeth at school.

"There you are," the woman shrills from down the hall, two or three doors down on the right. "Come inside!"

She scuttles into the doorway of the cafeteria room.

The voice comes through gently, a low hum at first that easily could be mistaken for the hospital life-flight helicopter. But it isn't. It's the beat and hum of something—of wings. I turn my body around facing the empty fifteen feet of hallway behind me, a window at its end, the door to the right—my room. I run fingers through my hair. My shoes fit and there are no footprints. The shoes still fit. The voice is sunlight and stars from the weeks passing. It's the farthest end of the hall and leaving by the second. I put a hand up to shade rays singled out there before me pointing an index finger to the brightness. I was chosen to be here?

Trembling, knees ready to buckle at any given time as if about to jump or fall, a cloud passes. The voice, it fades. Shade comes up and away over buildings, over skyscrapers and away. I am with it. I cup my hands to my face. Keeling over, I sob a river.

"Once things have settled down for him, he'll come home on visits. The doctor's going to start giving him a pass. This is special. First it will only be for an afternoon, then a day. Then a day and night. Eventually, he will be home for good. Or at least that's the plan."

"I see. Maybe I should wait until he asks for me, some random afternoon then?"

"Of course."

Group Journal Entry for Jim Nichols, room 903 dated June 25th

I woke up in the hall after that somehow, a part of me leaving with the morning to the sun. It was a strong moment not because I had to, was told to, or was burdened. It was a strong moment because it was my choice, my decision to do that, to leave that part of me behind me. I chose myself.

I am a billion tiny feathers.

Today I can't remember the room I had in college. I think it's the same room number I have here at the hospital because I requested it, room 203, after being here three weeks. They ask me why I want to switch rooms and roommates and, not telling them about the snoring, I simply say because I want to always find my way home. Sometimes a 9 is a 2. Sometimes people can go back in time.

"You think you're going to get lost here in the hall, Jim?"

"Not really. But a voice told me I belonged in room 203."

"Well, I know the main unit door has a lock and buzzer. Soon, you'll be able to walk the rest of the hospital with others to go to the gift shop or main cafeteria. If anything, we'll ask the gentlemen if they wouldn't mind the switch."

It's in the evening meditation group watching the videos with the silver-haired man talking about happiness and joy, trust and self-esteem, that Mary the Egyptian mother of four begins to tear up like a wound while all our eyes are closed near the end. I open mine to look.

She's burdened. Too many responsibilities at home she always said, too much to take care of. Her husband, her family, they asked her to come here. They ask so much of her. She misses her children.

I don't mind it, but close my eyes again and begin to think of sadness and what it really sounds or looks like. The room grows quiet except Mary and then someone else begins to cry. It's the nurse leading the exercise. I didn't know and she looks at me.

Dan, a few years older, keeps his eyes open the whole time looking at the three of us. I always thought he was looking out for everyone. He sits back and glares at the nurse, his eyes glass and arms folded. He judges her this way and I see it, leaning back on his chair's back two legs. Before the perfect judge, all will stand back. I close my eyes again and begin to cry.

"I'm sorry."

The Jewish kid has no idea what I'm talking about, so I speak up.

"I'm sorry about last week."

"What happened last week? I don't think anything's changed or you've done anything wrong."

I reach out my hand to him.

"My name is Jim and I think I have depression. How long do you expect to be here?"

"Not long. Thanks for the handshake, but I have to get back to my room."

He leaves to play pool with Patti. I sulk back to my room, staring outside the room's single-pane window. The doctor makes an afternoon visit. I never had an afternoon visit from him before.

"Good news, Jim. We're going to start getting you out a bit. You're able to go out with the others through the hospital on breaks."

"Thanks, Dr. Newman. Is something wrong?"

"No. What would make you say that?"

"It's afternoon. I'm beginning to remember things now, the times you've visited, the things I used to say or do. I feel bad I can't take some things back. Is that okay?"

"Yes, it is. It's normal. We can talk about it more at team."

I know about the team and wish I could go further. I wish I was a marathon.

In some cases, when medication and psychotherapy have not helped, a treatment known as electroconvulsive therapy (ECT) may be used. ECT uses a brief electrical current applied to the scalp while the patient is under anesthesia. The procedure takes about ten to fifteen minutes and patients typically receive ECT two to three times a week for a total of six to twelve treatments.

Team is a group of people, a panel of professionals assigned to me. To my close right, you see my social worker. To her right, my nurse whose input used to matter. He won't be at the next meeting. Across from him sits my patient care adviser who assures my patient rights, and on either side of her are one, Dr. Newman and two, my proctor from group. This is the team and they are facing us. They are interrogating, relentless and, above all, will keep me here forever if the mood so strikes them.

"You've all changed seats?"

"Yes, how did you know that, Jim?" asks Dr. Newman.

"Because I can't remember some of your names now. What are we going to talk about today?"

"Well, *you* of course. How have you been, Jim?"

"I've been good. I still want out of here. I don't see Patti Smith and there are newer people here now. Why are people coming and going and I'm not?"

"We just have to make sure you know who you are and what's happened to you since you came here. After today the team and I will be discussing if we'll be giving you home orders. It means you will be able to visit your family for the day. Your father has suggested your grandmother's house as a possible spot?"

"Is your grandmother close to you, or do you feel safe there?" the social worker asks.

"Yes, I think she's one of my best friends."

"Let's talk about friends. Have you been able to make any while you've been here?"

I want to tell the group proctor who comes into my room every day to shut up and leave me alone and leave the room. I bury the voice and thoughts, filter it, that which was exposed on the table with the team at feast.

"No, I don't want to know any of these crazy people. I want to be normal and treated normal. Did you know there's a guy Gary who talks to the wall in the hallway and shakes peoples' hands who aren't even there? Do you know how long he's been here? Patti Smith told me he's a 'lifer.'"

"Gary has schizophrenia, Jim. Do you know what that means? It means parts of the world he sees or thinks aren't real."

I want to ask if there are thoughts that aren't real then what can I believe in.

"Do you realize how far you've come? How much of your daily life has become real for you?"

"I know Gary is real."

"Well, I don't think you'll have to worry about that much longer, Jim. You can go back to your room now. It's almost lunch. What did you order?"

My mouth opens a bit.

"Something and it was good."

The dream I had before Dr. Dietrich woke me up for team this morning really woke me up. It was about Christa. She was walking alone on a beach, clouds gathering above her. On her island, you didn't expect the storms but there they were, the sun parting, dimness from the northwest and the sun drifting away from view.

"Okay, Rob."

She brings her hands to cover her eyes it's so bright. Then the voice inside me comes into booming audio. She would have to wait here until she could meet the voice and things could be good again.

The clouds swirled away. The voice goes. Christa drops to her knees into the sand. I wake up beside a woman in a lab coat.

"Christa, I don't think it's something to worry about. I'm sure Jim is going through some changes in there, but everything's going to be okay. His family says he will be coming home for a visit this Wednesday to his grandma's. They say not to bombard him, but that things will be okay."

"You're sure, Rob?"

She loved him. When I talked to him on the phone, the only time, his voice was hollow and weak like he was not there. I didn't tell Christa this. I told her his voice was booming and happy, that he missed her. I lied. I told her it was booming.

I call Christa and I can't tell if she's crying out of happiness or sadness, but she says she misses me more than life itself. I tell her I will be home soon in monotone. Hanging up the phone I am someone with a guillotine, an executioner at a French Revolution. The guillotine passes and falls.

"I think I just killed something."

Gary frantically tries to shake his invisible friend's hand, his sweaty palm and fingers going up and down, up and down again and again, nodding in approval. I shake my head and look down the corridor. The Jewish kid is practicing yoga in the phosphorescent hall lighting. Farther in the community room, Dan is watching Jerry Springer. A door or two from that, Mary is crying in a messy bed about being the shame of her family. She can be heard throughout the unit. Patti Smith is on the streets of Cleveland looking for the next heartbeat or pulse of rock n' roll explosion, alone in denim jacket and leather boots.

I had made some friends.

The STNA leads us down to a glassed-in garage room saying, "The hospital, of course."

I ask her if this were home and she chuckles, "If you want it to be."

Sitting in the vestibule, newspapers scatter and blow around by the evening wind. Dates pass that never were real. July and August. Baseball playoffs, back to school sales. I think of college and miss it. I miss everything bright.

He opened the door to the bathroom and came around the corner and I couldn't believe it was him.

"Mom, just look at your grandson, full of energy. Excited to go back to the hospital later? I'm sure there are a lot of people missing you, Jim."

"I don't know what's going on there, Dad. Can I sit on the couch for awhile?"

"Sure, Jimmy. We can talk later."

School. I want to know what happened to my grades.

"Jim, stop grinding your teeth like that. You'll wear them to nothing," Mom squeaks.

"I'm sorry, Grandma. I don't know what else to do with myself."

They have him on seven kinds of medication. Tonight, it drops to five. By the time we get Jim back he will be taking two regularly, a third for insomnia.

When Jim was admitted, I was sure it was schizophrenia. I knew he'd really been hurt. The first visit he asked about the voices. All I could do was tell him to keep fighting. I cried that afternoon in the covered hospital garage in my car. It rained outside. I didn't know where to go but knew I was leaving him. My son, braver now than a child, fights what lay under the bed, in the closet, the monster. Looking in the mirror did he ever think he was the monster?

"I love you, Jim. Things will get back to normal before you know it and I love you."

On my visit to Grandma's, I call my uncle and mother. I call my cousins and even Rob. Everyone asks how I am and I say good. Everything is good and I am alright. I am doing good.

"Jim, we're going start giving you passes to leave the unit to go on the grounds or the cafeteria by yourself. You just have to understand this comes with a lot of responsibility."

Dr. Newman is facing me. Half of the team aren't even here. Maybe they're not needed. He continues.

"You're going to be free to go soon, very soon. We'll have you visiting for two days and a night at home. What were your thoughts on your visit this week, Jim?"

"I was scared, Dr. Newman. I felt uneasy and like I didn't belong anymore."

"Well, I'm sure your family thinks you do. Your uncle will be picking you up tomorrow morning for your stay. We have only a few more steps and paperwork and you will be back out on your own again."

"Okay, Dr. Newman. May I be excused?"

I tuck my chair in properly, modestly, and politely.

"Yes, Jim. Have a good lunch."

I glance back on my way out of the doorway looking at the doctor, at myself in a new t-shirt, at the deconstructed team now three strong. I look up. I look away.

Searching for Patti, I walk through automatic back doors to the parking garage. I owe her something for nothing.

Dr. Newman doesn't know I take the trip. I take it for me. I've gotten the pass to go by myself and use it to the best of my ability to feel that way, to feel free. In the front vestibule are awnings guiding me out of the shadows above my head, unclasped and triggered to do so, glinting like the silver in the silver-haired man's scalp.

With the pass comes great responsibility.

I get to the bottom ramp of the garage fingering my soft pink plastic band. It's not ready to come off. The ink is smudged and illegible. I get to the edge of the garage at the sidewalk about to take a small right onto it when someone honks behind me, a red, four-door VW swerving jaggedly out. I'm on the parking garage ramp when Dr. Newman, on his way home, steps out.

In beekeeping, or apiculture, smoke calms bees, initiating a feeding response in anticipation of hive abandonment due to fire. Smoke also masks alarm pheromones released. The ensuing confusion creates an opportunity for a beekeeper to open a hive without triggering a defensive reaction. In addition, when a bee consumes honey the abdomen distends, supposedly making it difficult to make the necessary flexes to sting, though this has not been tested scientifically.

"I've still got my bracelet on. I'll find my way back. It's just a walk around the building," I tell him.

The street on the Upper East Side has vendors with flowers and hot dogs. I see construction signs and workers and think of Dan. I see a streetlight up close. I get to the sliding doors of the hospital and sit next to the flowerbed hearing the beat of Patti Smith's boots on Cleveland pavement fifteen miles due southwest, a low hum. I let go to the forward motion of surrendering what I cannot change through cage bars letting down their guard to a lesson and that yet to another lesson again. I keep that promise and they buzz me in.

"Jim, is that you?"

She is crying. Tears are rolling down her puffy, red cheeks. She doesn't even wipe or hide them. They roll away like saltwater from paddles, a boat at sea. She's alone there paddling to an island by herself. She's rowing, the way we rolled around in sleeping bags in her mother's backyard.

"Christa?"

The voice is shaky now. There is calm before the storm, the way clouds stretch themselves across the sky in thin lines warning of incoming fronts like jet streams, the way wind whispers through my uncle's cracked truck window.

"We may be able to kayak that someday. Don't you think, buddy?" he asks on the way here.

"Okay. At sea. An ocean kayak."

I couldn't even speak in full sentences.

I throw my arms around Christa the way it was meant to and taught to me by strangers. She sobs into my chest wiping the waves from the rowboat, left and right, snot into my t-shirt. She's been paddling all of this.

"I've missed you so much, Jim. I've missed you more than I can say."

I decide to describe it to her, holding her tighter with my hands at the shoulders and throwing my head back to see her face. I stretch my arms to their full reach and say it's okay. The scent of a perfume clouds us.

When a colony accidentally loses its queen, it is said to be 'queenless.' The workers realize the queen is absent in as little as an hour, her pheromones fading in the hive.

A colony cannot survive without a fertile queen laying eggs to renew the population, so workers select cells containing eggs aged less than three days, enlarging them dramatically to form 'emergency queen cells.' These appear similar to large peanut-like structures (about an inch long) which hang from the center or side of the combs. The developing larva in a queen cell is fed differently from ordinary worker bees, receiving the normal honey and pollen, but also a great deal of royal jelly, a special food secreted by young 'nurse bees' from a gland. This special food dramatically alters the growth and development of the larva. After metamorphosis and pupation, it emerges from the cell, a queen bee.

My uncle drives me back to the hospital the following afternoon and I don't know anyone there. There will be new people to fill the hall and ward, to do yoga and cry. I pass Dr. Newman and he obliges a hello. I repeat the same and he goes his way. I go mine. This is what it has come to. Dad stops in for lunch. He's off from work and checks me out at the main desk and we go to the Italian bistro across the street. He asks how I feel.

"Good, Dad. Things are changing and I'm feeling good about that."

It's the first time I've been able to say something other than 'okay' about how I feel to someone.

"You know your girlfriend's beautiful, Jim. How did you feel about seeing her?"

I hesitate like a recoup through a conversation just like this, switching weight in the booth to the other leg.

"Yes, she is."

"Is there anything else you'd like to say about her, Jim?" he asks.

Our meal arrives. I've ordered a turkey melt at an Italian restaurant. The waitress refills my drink and I've slurped it to nothing. There is nothing to say.

"Not at the moment, Dad. Can we just eat?"

And this is how to win at a war, Sun Tzu.

She moves over me, takes control, and submits. I kiss her mouth, the opening like a cave-heart. My heart is empty. She is with me when she reaches the island. Cold winter coming, her hair like twigs and bare branches.

We're in the upstairs of her mom's barn, once a work garage for carpentry, automobiles, practicing love. There are artist and photography books stored here from the seventies when her mother took up painting. I wish I could see the boat to shore, drag it through the seaweed and sand. Old lamps light the way on how to practice making love even though it's daylight. It's time that separates us and time that forgets our humanity. We stand in repose. She sees the clouds now, I can tell. I see them, too. I kiss her forehead with something in her eyes staring back at me—the eye of a storm, the trouble and the dark. It's so dark here. It's so cold. Her eyes reflect the world of what is left in the past when falling out of love.

Storms haunt me.

I paddle the rowboat away from the island and do not look back. I look forward. I do not wave for lack of a spare hand. I row in panicked resolve, shoulder over shoulder, each stroke looking down with a brow of sweat and tears filling the boat for the light left behind me. The missive, it is Christa.

It begins to rain, drops bombarding the barn's tin roof. We are at war. We are at fault and without faith. It is civil. It's the last stand in a series of stands. I look down under my breath saying goodbye the way I say to Dr. Newman, to Gary, to my voice somewhere on a sunbeam. There is no light there.

Goodbye, Christa.

"We're going to release you, Jim."

"What do you mean? I'll be free to come and go now?"

"Jim, this is a place of impermanence. This is a transition. Do you still have your copy of that poem

I gave you so long ago? Did you ever take the time to read it?"

"Yes, Dr. Newman. It's in my room in the unit in my packed bag. Do you need it back? I can give it back to you if you need it."

"Jim, your papers will be ready by the end of the day and your dad will be picking you up. There will be check-ups with me for medications and well-being as well as an assigned counselor from the hospital medical system. I have carried you as far as I can."

I fold the leg over the other, swaying at the nurses' desk flirting with some of them. This will be the last day I will see them, I say. The redheaded nurse says great and I ask if she means that she will be glad to see me go. She is the one who led our meditation group and says, "No. It's great that you have recovered, Jim."

The doctor gives me the papers. The battle is won, a static announcement from over the hospital public address system, a code or fire drill, shrilling. We never leave for those. Just imagine so many crazies on the street.

"The battle has just begun," it squawks.

I look over my discharge papers for the first time in the car ride home. They are green carbon copies. Dad looks at them. He teases my blonde, somewhat longer hair. I've achieved something. I hadn't graduated, but I'd achieved something. And I don't look at them again and won't for three days. When I do, it's to reread the line over and over again: Bi-Polar Depression I w/ Signs of Psychosis. It's in cursive with no period and signed by the doctor. A copy sent to the dean, I keep this one for a few years. It stays in a shoebox with my medications until I all but forget to use them. I try. I do and do not give up.

"He left me. He literally just left me." Scratching my chin coaxing it to understand the situation wiping and fiddling with the top of my head, the place that will be bald in ten years, and still the answer isn't there. Thoughts come forward and back again and there's nowhere to walk away from this.

"I don't understand," I say naively.

"He said he wasn't sure if he loved me anymore, Rob. After two months of waiting for him while he's in there and he leaves me. I love him."

She starts sobbing. I want this to be black and white like an old movie. I throw arms half-heartedly around her saying he needs time. We fold our heads lightly onto each other's shoulders.

"You knew this didn't you? You knew this would happen!"

Words come out like coyote shouts, animal moans meant for dusk and longing. I didn't know this would happen. I'd barely gotten a chance to see him since he'd been gone and back with his uncle. It probably wasn't the best that I invited Christa to the cookout. It probably wasn't the best that I had no answer for her. And just like that: blank, white paper. I tell her to write the thoughts down, let them explain things to him. I offer her a napkin, though it's not much to write with, and she wipes her face. I almost see a smile.

"I left her last week, Rob."

"I know, but she's already with me in the gas station cleaning up. I have no choice. I hope you see that."

"Then we'll get through this and roll with it, friend." I hang up the phone and search the apartment with my eyes.

"He's bringing Christa, Uncle Dave. She sounds like a whole mess, but he's bringing her. I don't know if I can get through this. I feel so frail coming from the hospital a week ago. What should I do?"

"Eat," he says.

He goes to the balcony lifting the iron lid, a plume of smoke from a past barbecue cascading from the unkept grill and hiding his face. He slides the glass-paned door behind him. I doubt going back the way I'd come. The television in the living room shows a movie on DVD that my uncle owns and I wonder where the community room is, the red-headed nurse, Dan. A car door shuts as do my eyes—painfully. I hear a motor short on oil ping, come idle, then shut off. Another door shuts, not as loud, but it shuts. Doors are closing around me.

"Just get it," Uncle Dave says, sliding the balcony glass back shut again.

The movie is paused. Her lower lip trembles as she walks past me into the room and beyond to the couch. There is weight in the room and a setting for four at the table. We have ways and means and I'm afraid of the pattern we will sit in.

Uncle Dave comes in from the balcony and sets a platter of meat on the table, patting Rob on the back. She is quiet and manages a whimper here and there, rearranging her food on the plate while not eating much. When she lets out a final sigh, napkins are dirty on all plates but hers. There's a pair of brussel sprouts, a cold steak left pointing to them like a constellation.

We used to be a pair.

I ask her if she wants to go on the balcony to talk. She goes, draped in the moment like a willow tree or dark dress. I tell her she has to eat, has to get over everything. She obliges, but says she doesn't understand why. She cries some. We exit, lights fading to black. Uncle Dave and Rob fade. Happiness that once was, it fades, too. The curtain falls and there is applause.

"She's still having a hard time dealing with it."

I doubted I'd ever go back to the college again. I've applied to the local community college for Fall and take a single class there, a foreign language.

Rob and I walk out of my grandmother's front door taking a left to head down to the square past the library, the courthouse and jail on up into north town where all the businesses are. We watch a movie at the theater there, a matinee. It's about a group of friends struggling in their early twenties to define themselves. Music plays a role.

This will be the last time I see Rob. It will be the last time we ever truly talk about Christa or her well-being. I am sad, but not because I know this. I tell him some jokes I learned in the unit and he laughs. Still, I don't talk too much or too loudly about what happened there.

When I return from the trip, he'll have begun dating someone while I continue to wash dishes at the restaurant, living with Grandma and going to the class. We set out from here and I tell her about my decision to go to Florida.

"I understand, Jimmy," she says.

I tell her I want to make sure I've made the right decisions in my life. More importantly, I want to prove that I can do this.

A night tide comes up to my tent. Poor beaches in the Keys are a mixture of the coral reef and imported sand. I hear pitter patters, gently hugging a bottle of wine closer, and fall asleep this way. The next morning, I rent a bicycle for coffee shops, a Cuban art gallery, and Hemingway's house. I read. It is a language I understand. When I have the courage to call home, it's only Rob who answers my call. He asks if I'm okay, says how my family is a bit worried, at least my dad. He asks if he can date Christa. I pause, say yes, and he is glad. I tell him I am, too. I hang up the phone, getting back on the bike and I head to the dock.

Street performers set up at dusk here going on generations. Looking over my shoulder on the boardwalk, the sun sets brilliantly on their faces behind. I think of Gary as one stops juggling to cup hands to his forehead on an island I had finally found.